Dear Parent:
Your child's love of readi

Every child learns to read in a different way and at his own speed. Some go back and forth between reading levels and read favorite books again and again. Others read through each level in order. You can help your young reader improve and become more confident by encouraging his or her own interests and abilities. From books your child reads with you to the first books he or she reads alone, there are I Can Read Books for every stage of reading:

SHARED READING
Basic language, word repetition, and whimsical illustrations, ideal for sharing with your emergent reader

BEGINNING READING
Short sentences, familiar words, and simple concepts for children eager to read on their own

READING WITH HELP
Engaging stories, longer sentences, and language play for developing readers

READING ALONE
Complex plots, challenging vocabulary, and high-interest topics for the independent reader

I Can Read Books have introduced children to the joy of reading since 1957. Featuring award-winning authors and illustrators and a fabulous cast of beloved characters, I Can Read Books set the standard for beginning readers.

A lifetime of discovery begins with the magical words **"I Can Read!"**

Visit www.icanread.com for information
on enriching your child's reading experience.

My Little Pony: Pony Life: Meet the Ponies

HASBRO and its logo, MY LITTLE PONY and all related characters are trademarks of Hasbro and are used with
permission. © 2021 Hasbro.
All Rights Reserved. Printed in the United States of America.
No part of this book may be used or reproduced in any manner whatsoever without written permission
except in the case of brief quotations embodied in critical articles and reviews. For information address
HarperCollins Children's Books, a division of HarperCollins Publishers, 195 Broadway, New York, NY 10007.
www.icanread.com

Library of Congress Control Number: 2020946932
ISBN 978-0-06-303744-1

Book design by Elaine Lopez-Levine

22 23 24 25 LSCC 10 9 8 7 6 5 4 3 ❖ First Edition

My First SHARED READING · I Can Read!

MY LITTLE PONY

PONY LIFE

Meet the Ponies

HARPER

An Imprint of HarperCollins*Publishers*

Meet the ponies!

A pony life is full
of magic and friendship.

Meet Twilight Sparkle.
She has magic powers.
And she loves to read.

Twilight Sparkle's friends
are important to her.

Meet Pinkie Pie!
She is the silliest pony.
She makes every
pony smile!

Pinkie Pie owns a bakery!
Her friends love her
cupcakes.

Meet Rainbow Dash!

She has wings.

She loves racing.

Rainbow Dash is a great
flyer.

She is also a great friend!

Meet Rarity!

She is one of a kind.

She loves fashion.

Rarity has a big heart.

She always helps her friends.

Meet Fluttershy!

She is sweet and kind.

She loves animals.

Fluttershy enjoys being
home with her friends.

Meet Applejack!
You can trust her.
She is honest
with everypony.

Applejack will offer
a helping hoof.
She always knows
what to do!

The ponies love having fun!

They solve problems.

They have adventures.

They laugh together.

They are friends forever!